Little
Ripper
Reads

Bad Luck

The Five Mile Press

The Five Mile Press

The Five Mile Press Pty Ltd
950 Stud Road, Rowville Victoria 3178
Australia
Phone 61 3 8756 5500
Fax   61 3 8756 5588
Email: publishing@fivemile.com.au

First published 2003

Text © Chris McTrustry
Text and cover design by Lucy Adams
Paged by Lucy Adams
Illustrated by Mitch Vane
Edited by Catherine Green

Printed in China

National Library of Australia
Cataloguing-in-Publication data

McTrustry, Chris.
    Bad Luck.

    For children.
    ISBN 1 74124 022 0.

    1. Fairies - Juvenile fiction. 2. Wishes - Juvenile
    fiction. I. Vane, Mitch. II. Title. (Series : Little
    ripper reads).

A823.3

Little Ripper Reads

Bad Luck

Chris McTrustry

Illustrated by Mitch Vane

The Five Mile Press

Make Sure YOU Catch These Little Ripper Reads!

The Spider
That Barked

An adventure by Helen Chapman

Fridays Are
Doomed

A humorous story by Alison Reynolds

Contents

Chapter 1

The Return of Bad Luck

The night Agatha Cooper's father was changed into a roast lamb dinner signalled the return of Bad Luck, the wish fairy. Once a year, Bad Luck visited the town of Bad Luck (named in his dishonour) and granted three wishes. But they were *bad* wishes.

Now, Mr Cooper knew how dangerous Bad Luck could be. However, while fumbling for his house key, he sniffed the liver Mrs Cooper was preparing for dinner.

'Why can't we have roast lamb for dinner?' he groaned. 'Roast lamb with vegetables and gravy. What else could a person wish for?'

POOF! One roast lamb dinner.

You see, Bad Luck, naughty creature, didn't grant Mr Cooper his *exact* wish.

And who should be waiting at the front door for his master, but Rollo, the Coopers' dog?

GOBBLE!

Agatha witnessed this event from her bedroom window. She rushed down to the front door and shooed Rollo away, but all that was left of her father were two pieces of broccoli.

Later, Agatha told the authorities that Bad Luck had returned. Although she was just a child, she vowed to meet Bad Luck and get her father back. So, she wandered Bad Luck's streets with one wish: to meet Bad Luck.

The townsfolk of Bad Luck couldn't believe their ears. No one had ever wished to meet Bad Luck.

At first, the townsfolk were worried about this confused girl. But then, some were heard to say: 'Let her call Bad Luck. Then it will leave us alone.'

At breakfast on the second day of Bad Luck's visit, a crowd of newspaper reporters gathered outside the Cooper house.

'Is the confused girl all right?' a reporter called to Mrs Cooper.

'Has her wish been granted?' called another reporter.

'Yes and no,' Mrs Cooper replied. 'And my daughter isn't confused. She is brave!'

Then she slammed the door!

'That's telling them, Mother,' Agatha said.

'Oh, be quiet, you confused girl!' snapped Mrs Cooper.

'B-but, you just said ...' began Agatha.

'My dear,' said Mrs Cooper.
'Chasing Bad Luck is dangerous.
Let others do it.'

'Everyone is scared of Bad Luck,'
Agatha replied. 'It has to be me!'

Chapter 2

Bad Luck Appears

Agatha spent the day marching up and down Bad Luck's streets, bravely wishing her special wish. But Bad Luck did not appear. As night fell and darkness closed in, Mrs Cooper took Agatha home.

Agatha wished her wish all the way home.

And Agatha wished her wish
while she was in the bath.

And while she dressed for bed.

And while she brushed her teeth. But Bad Luck did not appear.

'Bad Luck *must* have heard my wish,' she said to her mother.

Mrs Cooper smiled. 'What you're doing is brave. But I think Bad Luck likes its victims to be less ... hostile.' She kissed Agatha on the forehead. 'Good night, my dear.'

Agatha was soon fast asleep, dreaming of Bad Luck.

Just on sunrise, a creaking floorboard woke Agatha. There was someone, or perhaps something, in her bedroom.

Agatha held her breath. Slowly, she sat up and peered into the early morning light. A small boy sat perched on her toy box. Thin shafts of light caught his bright green eyes that darted hither and thither, dancing with mischief.

'I got your message,' the small boy with green eyes said.

'You're Bad Luck?' Agatha spluttered.

'The one and only.' Bad Luck sneered. 'What do you want?'

'I want to talk to you!'

'Talk?' Bad Luck gurgled. 'What, no wish?'

'That's right,' Agatha said. 'You turned my father into ... into ... something he shouldn't be. And I want him back!'

Chapter 3

Bad Luck Tells His Story

Bad Luck stared at Agatha. 'You can't talk to me like that!'

'You have a gift, but it's being wasted,' Agatha sighed.

'No!' Bad Luck replied. 'People waste my gift. I used to grant happy wishes. But no one appreciated them. It was always "give me this", never a thought for others.'

'You?' Agatha said, 'Grant people happy wishes!'

'Yes, and people gave me gifts, too. I haven't always been a Wish Fairy, you horrid oink!' shouted Bad Luck. 'I used to be a human boy. Because of me, my parents became bankrupt – they had no money. We used to live in town in a fine white house, with a red roof and five chimneys.'

'I know that house,' Agatha said. 'Now, it's a –'

'That's not important,' snapped Bad Luck. 'Because I brought it all to an end.'

Bad Luck sounded very sad.

'I was always wishing for a new something. A toy. A game. My parents spent all their money trying to please me. I wished them broke! And to grant other people their wishes, forever, is my punishment!'

Bad Luck started to cry. Agatha gently patted his shoulder.

'Don't cry,' she said. 'I'm sure I can help you.'

'Oh really?' whined Bad Luck. 'What makes you so sure you can help me?'

Agatha smiled. 'I have A Really Good Idea. And it's simple. You must grant me another wish.'

'I knew it!' Bad Luck said. 'You're worse than the rest. You want two wishes!'

Agatha sighed. 'Silly Wish Fairy. I –'

'Silly, am I?' huffed Bad Luck. 'We'll see who's silly. Goodbye!'

And before Agatha could say another word, like 'sorry', Bad Luck vanished.

Chapter 4
A Surprise for Agatha

At breakfast the next morning, Agatha told her mother what had happened.

'Well, you can't give up now,' Mrs Cooper said.

'But,' Agatha replied, 'you said Bad Luck was dangerous.'

Mrs Cooper smiled. 'You spoke to him and survived. I think your plan will work.'

'Well,' Agatha said, 'I won't give up.'

After breakfast, Agatha and her mother hurried out into the town. Agatha had found Bad Luck once, maybe she could do it again.

Although she wished herself blue in the face, Agatha had no luck.

As late afternoon became early evening, Mrs Cooper said it was time to go home.

'You've done all you can,' Mrs Cooper said to Agatha.

'But I can't give up yet,' sobbed Agatha.

'Sometimes, you have to give up,' Mrs Cooper said softly as she put her arms around her daughter. 'Let's go home, Agatha.'

A surprise greeted Agatha when she and her mother arrived home.

'They're the Mayor's horses,' Mrs Cooper said.

The Mayor had come to visit Agatha to tell her some special news. He cleared his throat and said: 'As the only citizen in the history of Bad Luck to challenge the Wish Fairy –'

'Excuse me, Mr Mayor,' Mrs Cooper said. 'But, Agatha spoke to the Wish Fairy this morning.'

The Mayor turned pale. 'S-s-spoke to Bad Luck.' He continued: 'And survived?'

Agatha shrugged. 'He's really just an unhappy little boy.'

But the Mayor wasn't listening. His face now beamed in a broad smile.

'You spoke to Bad Luck and survived, little girl! My, my. You really are a heroine. An example to us all! We shall stage a civic reception for you, Agatha Cooper. You will receive the town's highest bravery award.'

'Not the Golden Sabre!' Mrs Cooper gasped.

'The very same,' the Mayor said. 'And you shall receive it tonight.'

As the Mayor headed for his horses, he said: 'I must return to the Town Hall and put on my finest robes. This is an important night for Bad Luck!'

Chapter 5

An Important Night for Bad Luck

'Awards are all very fine,' Agatha said, planting her hands on her hips. 'But I've still got a Wish Fairy to defeat!'

'I'm so proud of you, Agatha,' Mrs Cooper said. 'If only your father was here ...' And a tear trickled down her cheek.

For a little while, Agatha and her mother forgot about Bad Luck. They had to get ready for the award ceremony.

There were clothes to iron and shoes to shine. There was also hair to tease and just a little bit of make-up to apply.

Then, quickly, as there wasn't really a moment to spare before the ceremony, Agatha and her mother got dressed and hurried off to the Town Hall.

The Town Hall was decked out with bright streamers and banners. Spotlights shone into the night sky. But there were no people. Anywhere.

The Mayor greeted Agatha and her mother warmly.

'Where is –?' Mrs Cooper began.

'Everyone thinks you are brave, Agatha,' the Mayor explained. 'But they are still frightened of Bad Luck.' He opened the door of the Town Hall. 'Come in. We're ready to start the award ceremony.'

Mrs Cooper started up the steps, but stopped when she realised Agatha wasn't beside her.

'Hurry up, Agatha,' she said.

But Agatha stayed where she
was – at the bottom of the steps,
statue-like, staring.

'Mother,' she said, looking at Mrs Cooper. 'I know where Bad Luck lives.'

'Where?' asked Mrs Cooper.

And Agatha pointed to the Library, which was next door to the Town Hall. Bad Luck's library was a fine white brick building, with a red roof and five chimneys.

'This is Bad Luck's home. Or at least it used to be,' Agatha said.

'Where are you going, little girl?' asked the Mayor as Mrs Cooper walked down the steps to her daughter.

Agatha turned and said to the Mayor: 'Please understand, Mr Mayor. I must do something very important. It will help our town. I will return.'

And with that, she and her
mother hurried inside the Library.

'Where do we start looking?'
asked Mrs Cooper.

'Let's try the Children's Section,'
Agatha said. 'Follow me.'

They hurried to the Children's
Section, but there was no one there.

Agatha called to Bad Luck:

'Please come out!'

No answer.

Agatha sighed. 'Oh, come out,
you silly boy!'

'What do you want?' said a voice
behind them. They spun around.
Bad Luck slouched against the
doorway.

'Is this Bad Luck?' Mrs Cooper asked, sounding very surprised and not at all afraid.

'Yes,' Agatha replied. 'Remember to empty your mind of thoughts.'

'Of course,' Mrs Cooper said.

Agatha turned to Bad Luck and smiled warmly. 'You left before I could tell you my wish.'

Bad Luck curled his lip and folded his arms. 'I'm not interested,' he said.

'You will be,' replied Agatha.

Suddenly, Bad Luck smiled mischievously. 'I believe someone is wishing ...'

54

Chapter 6
The Best Wish

'Mother!' Agatha yelled. 'Don't think of anything!'

'Too late,' Bad Luck giggled. 'Someone is wishing!' He pointed at Mrs Cooper.

'Wait,' Agatha pleaded. 'I know how to set you free.'

'How?' Bad Luck asked.

'Please grant me one last wish,' Agatha begged.

'No!' Bad Luck cried. 'You've had your wish. No more wishes for you.'

'Listen to me!' Agatha said. She faced Bad Luck. 'I wish Bad Luck had never been made a Wish Fairy. I wish, with all my heart, that he had stayed a little boy!'

Bad Luck looked at Agatha with happy eyes. 'That truly is A Really Good Idea! Wish granted!'

There was a blinding flash, then silence. Bad Luck had disappeared.

'Did it work?' Mrs Cooper asked.

Agatha shrugged and said,

'I don't know.'

Suddenly, the rows of books in the Children's Section of Bad Luck's Library started to disappear. Then the bookshelves faded away, one by one.

'What's happening?' Mrs Cooper cried, holding Agatha tightly.

'Excuse me,' said an old voice from behind them. 'What are you doing in my house?' An old man shuffled into the room. He was short and his green eyes danced with mischief.

'You look familiar,' he said to Agatha. 'Have we met before?'

Agatha knew at once who the old man was – and who he had been.

'Once, a long time ago, we met each other,' she smiled. She looked around at the beautiful furniture that had replaced the bookshelves. 'Your home is very lovely.'

The old man smiled. 'I have everything I wish for, except … '

Agatha stepped forward. 'Would you like it if we visited you?'

'I would be delighted!' replied the old man.

And his green eyes danced with
happiness as he hugged Agatha.

Outside, the Town Hall stood in darkness. There were no decorations or spotlights.

'What are we doing here?' asked a puzzled Mrs Cooper.

'I'm not sure.' Agatha shook her head. She vaguely remembered a boy who caused mischief. Then she remembered all that had happened, but she said nothing. She just smiled.

'Let's go home,' Mrs Cooper said. 'Your father will be waiting for his roast lamb dinner!'

Chris McTrustry

I've always liked telling stories.
I enjoy a good laugh as well, so I
always try to get a little humour
into my stories. The idea of a
genie (or wish granter) who gives
people bad wishes instead of
good ones made me smile. This
story is the result of that idea and
that smile.

Mitch Vane

I think I caught the drawing
bug from my mother. I used to
watch her draw and paint as
I was growing up. I work from
home in a studio overlooking
the garden. I like to use
watercolour and a scratchy dip
pen in my artwork. I am a very
messy worker – my clothes and
fingers are ALWAYS covered
in ink.